P9-BBV-488

CAROLE LEXA SCHAEFER

SNOW PUMPKIN

ILLUSTRATED BY PIERR MORGAN

CROWN PUBLISHERS ❧ NEW YORK

For my forever friends, Connie and Marcia,
and for Tracy—editor extraordinaire
—C.L.S.

For Tracy and Carole,
and for Max
—P.M.

Text copyright © 2000 by Carole Lexa Schaefer
Illustrations copyright © 2000 by Pierr Morgan

Published by Crown Publishers, a division of Random House, Inc.
CROWN and colophon are trademarks of Random House, Inc.

www.randomhouse.com/kids

Library of Congress Cataloging-in-Publication Data
Schaefer, Carole Lexa.
Snow Pumpkin / by Carole Lexa Schaefer; illustrated by Pierr Morgan. — 1st ed.
p. cm.
Summary: When it snows in October, two friends build a snowman
using a pumpkin as its head.
[1. Snow—Fiction. 2. Snowmen—Fiction. 3. Pumpkin—Fiction.]
I. Morgan, Pierr, ill. II. Title.
PZ7.S3315 Sn 2000
[E]—dc21 00-022658
ISBN 0-517-80015-2 (trade)
       0-517-80016-0 (lib. bdg.)

Printed in Singapore

10 9 8 7 6 5 4 3 2 1
September 2000
First Edition

Night before last, when the first snow fell,
Gram was the one who couldn't believe it.
"Too early," she said. "It's still October."

I poked my arm outside and pulled it back in.
Snowflakes sparkled on my pajama sleeve.

We hurried to look at them—every one different—
through Gram's reading glass.

Next morning, a little pillow of snow
rested on my window sill.
I measured it with Gram's sewing tape: three inches.
"Yippee! Enough to build a snowman," I said.
"Maybe," said Gram.

After breakfast, all bundled up,
I scrunched through the snow
across the street and up the hill
to the park.

At the bike rack, I said hello
to Mr. Rhee and his Scottie dog.
"Those bikes won't go out today," Mr. Rhee said.
"Too tired." He winked. "Get it? *Bi*-cycles? *Two*-tired?"

I laughed all the way up the hill to where
my friend Jesse stood by the shaggy trees.
"Look, Lily," he said. "Every branch has a snow hat on."
"Nice," I said, and pulled him along to Snowman Square.

"It's too crowded," said Jesse. "Where's the snow for *us?*"
I made two snowballs and gave Jesse one.
"Follow me," I said.

We zigged and zagged around everybody, rolling up snow

until we got to the other side of the square.

Together, we packed our snow lumps into a body.
"We don't have enough for a head," said Jesse.

So Jesse and I rolled snow again,
slipping and sliding across the park,
all the way to the community garden
where Gram and I have our vegetable patch.

Jesse held up the snowball.

"It's all full of grass and stuff," he said.

"Not so good," I said. "But look at my pumpkins, Jesse."

They showed in the snow as bright as three orange suns.
"Hey!" yelled Jesse. "The middle one has a face."
He was right.

Jesse and I carried that pumpkin to the square
and put it up on our snowman.

Lots of people looked at it and danced around it with
Jesse and me until it was time for us to go home.

I told Gram, "You have to come and see
the snow pumpkin man we made."
"Tomorrow," she said.

This morning, the sun came out.
It melted the snow on my window sill
and made it drip-drop down like tears
until I felt like crying myself.

Jesse sloshed over to our place
and knocked on the door.
"Come on, Gram," I said.
"We have to go to the park *right now*."

In the square, Gram and Jesse and I
found our pumpkin sitting in a snowy puddle.
"Oh dear," said Gram.
"It's all melted!" cried Jesse.
"But not all gone," I said.
"Our Snow Pumpkin's still here."

We took it home.

This afternoon, Jesse and I made
snowflakes—every one different.
We hung them in the window
all around Snow Pumpkin,

who sits on the sill this October night . . .

. . . and smiles.